BUGS UP CLOSE!

GRASSHOPPERS UP CLOSE

RACHAEL MORLOCK

PowerKiDS press.
New York

Published in 2020 by The Rosen Publishing Group, Inc.
29 East 21st Street, New York, NY 10010

First Edition

Editor: Elizabeth Krajnik
Book Design: Michael Flynn

Photo Credits: Cover, p. 1 jordeangjelovik/Shutterstock.com; (series background) Karuka/Shutterstock.com; pp. 5, 19 Keith Michael Taylor/Shutterstock.com; p. 7 Krysja/Shutterstock.com; p. 9 Paulo Melo/Shutterstock.com; p. 11 anat chant/Shutterstock.com; p. 13 Sonja Weakley/Shutterstock.com; p. 15 Dmytro Khlystun/Shutterstock.com; p. 17 NEFS/Shutterstock.com; p. 21 Geza Farkas/Shutterstock.com; p. 22 livestock99/Shutterstock.com.

Cataloging-in-Publication Data

Names: Morlock, Rachael.
Title: Grasshoppers up close / Rachael Morlock.
Description: New York : PowerKids Press, 2020. | Series: Bugs up close! | Includes glossary and index.
Identifiers: ISBN 9781725307902 (pbk.) | ISBN 9781725307926 (library bound) | ISBN 9781725307919 (6 pack)
Subjects: LCSH: Grasshoppers--Juvenile literature.
Classification: LCC QL508.A2 M667 2020 | DDC 595.7'26--dc23

Manufactured in the United States of America

CPSIA Compliance Information: Batch #CWPK20. For Further Information contact Rosen Publishing, New York, New York at 1-800-237-9932.

CONTENTS

Grasshoppers Galore

Grasshoppers are a kind of **insect**. There are more than 11,000 species, or kinds, of grasshoppers. They are most often brown, but they can be yellowish brown, reddish brown, light green, or striped. Grasshoppers' colors may help them find **mates** or warn away predators.

From Egg to Adult

All grasshoppers begin life as tiny eggs. When an egg hatches, the tiny wingless grasshopper that comes out is called a nymph. Nymphs grow over time and **shed** their **exoskeleton**. This is called molting. Grasshoppers molt about five times before becoming adults and growing wings.

Parts of a Grasshopper

Grasshoppers have three main parts: a head, a thorax, and an abdomen. Their head has antennae, **compound eyes**, and ocelli, which are a type of simple eye that senses movement. The grasshopper's mouthparts help bring food to its mouth and help it chew.

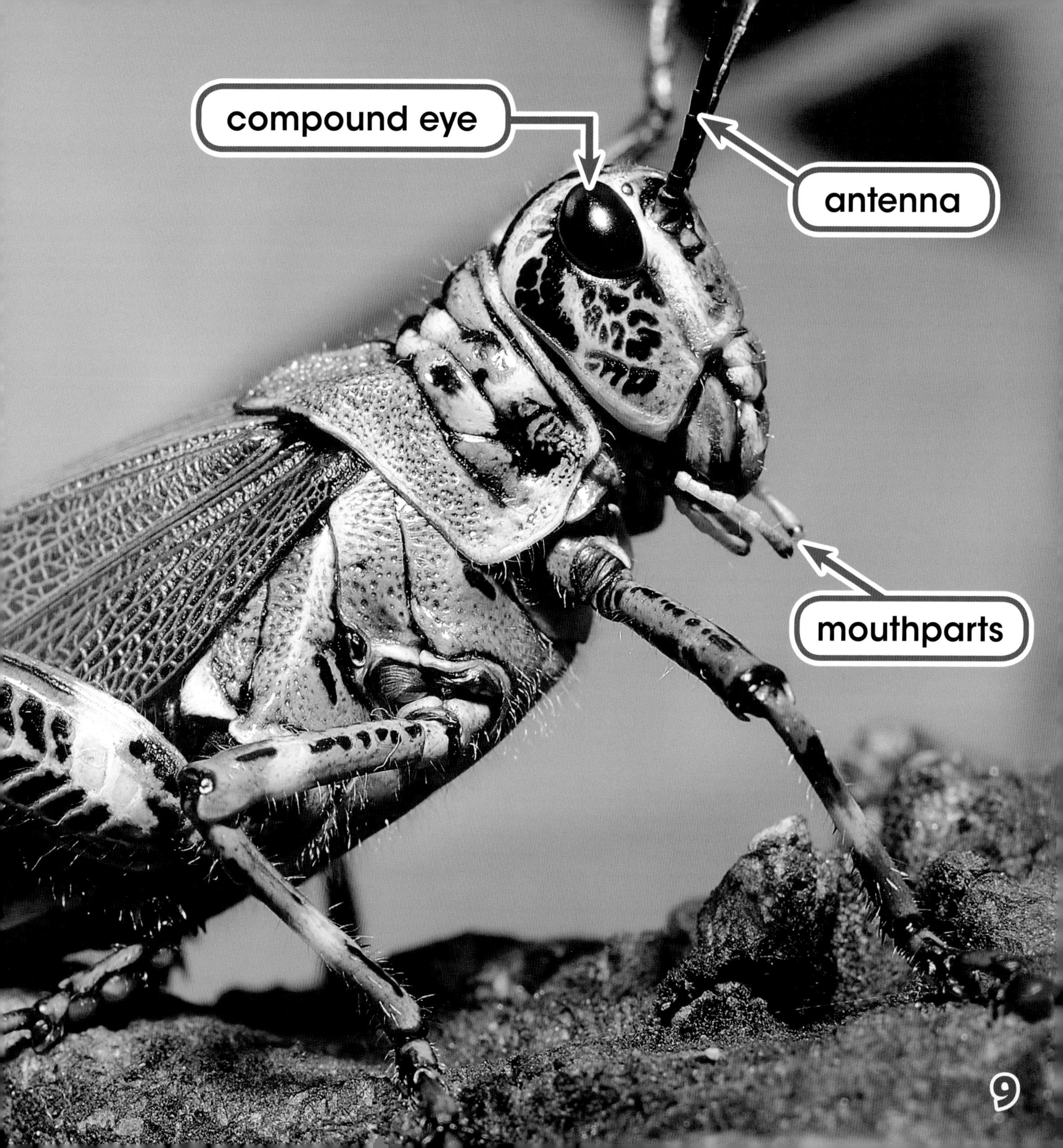
compound eye
antenna
mouthparts

The Thorax

The grasshopper's middle part is called the thorax. This is where the grasshopper's three pairs of legs and two pairs of wings are. The first pair of wings is usually smaller and lies over the second pair of wings.

thorax
leg
wing

Long Wings

The grasshopper's two pairs of wings are different sizes, do different jobs, and are different shapes. The front pair is skinny and somewhat hard. The back pair is larger and more flexible, or able to bend. Some scientists study wing **veins** to tell what species a grasshopper is.

Strong Legs

Grasshoppers have three pairs of legs. Their back legs are much larger then the front two pairs. The back legs have large **muscles** to push them off the ground and into the air. Some grasshoppers can jump 20 times the length of their body!

Making Music

Male grasshoppers make a kind of music to get females to notice them. They rub their back legs quickly up and down against their front wings. This makes a sound. Some grasshoppers may also rub their wings together to make noise.

The Abdomen

The grasshopper's end part is called the abdomen. It's made up of many joined parts. The abdomen is flexible so the grasshopper can breathe, mate, and lay eggs. The grasshopper's abdomen is where the parts that break down food and make babies are.

abdomen

On the Food Chain

Most grasshoppers are herbivores, which means they eat only plants. They live in fields, meadows, or other places with leaves and grasses to feed on. Grasshoppers have to stay away from predators who want to eat them or their eggs. These predators include birds, frogs, snakes, flies, and even humans!

Grasshoppers All Over!

Grasshoppers are found around the world, except for the very cold areas around the North Pole and South Pole. They live in many types of places, including deserts, forests, and grasslands. Keep an eye out for grasshoppers where you live!

GLOSSARY

compound eye: An eye made up of hundreds of lenses that make one picture in the brain.

exoskeleton: A hard outer covering on an animal.

insect: A small animal that has six legs and a body formed of three parts and that may have wings.

mate: To come together to make babies, or one of two animals that come together to make babies.

muscle: A part of the body that produces motion.

shed: To lose or cast aside a natural covering or part.

vein: A tube in the body that carries blood back to the heart.

INDEX

WEBSITES

Due to the changing nature of Internet links, PowerKids Press has developed an online list of websites related to the subject of this book. This site is updated regularly. Please use this link to access the list: www.powerkidslinks.com/buc/grasshoppers

INSIDER TIPS FOR HUNTING TURKEY

XINA M. UHL AND
KATE CANINO

New York

Published in 2019 by The Rosen Publishing Group, Inc.
29 East 21st Street, New York, NY 10010

First Edition

Library of Congress Cataloging-in-Publication Data

Names: Uhl, Xina M., author. | Canino, Kate, author.
Title: Insider tips for hunting turkey / Xina M. Uhl and Kate Canino.
Description: New York : Rosen Central, 2019. | Series: The ultimate guide to hunting | Includes bibliographical references and index. | Audience: Grades 5–8.
Identifiers: LCCN 2017048352| ISBN 9781508181835 (library bound) | ISBN 9781508181842 (pbk.)
Subjects: LCSH: Turkey hunting—Juvenile literature.
Classification: LCC SK325.T8 U35 2018 | DDC 799.2/4645—dc23
LC record available at https://lccn.loc.gov/2017048352

Manufactured in the United States of America

CONTENTS

INTRODUCTION

Humans have hunted since the dawn of time. Prior to the modern era, getting enough food to eat was of major concern to most people, who had to contend with bad weather, famines, droughts, diseases, and other disasters affecting their food supply. Hunting animals for food allowed people to survive, and though in most places today the practice of hunting is no longer necessary, it is still an activity that many people find challenging, enjoyable, and fulfilling. It connects hunters with nature in a way that they may not experience in their daily lives and provides friends and family members with time spent together in a time-tested, meaningful way.

As many people become more concerned with food quality and the use of hormones and antibiotics in farm-raised turkeys, wild turkeys provide a delicious protein source free of these substances. Animal welfare is also a concern of many people, especially at a time where the National Turkey Foundation reports that at least forty-six million farm-raised turkeys are consumed on the Thanksgiving holiday alone. Wild turkeys have lives free of cramped quarters and industrial production facilities that most of these birds endure.

Turkey hunters are included in the more than eleven million hunters that took to the fields in 2016, according to the U.S. Fish & Wildlife Service. For those who want to join the ranks of turkey hunters—or those who already have—this guide provides up-to-date, helpful information on turkey habitats and behavior, preparing for a hunt, the use and care of firearms and other weapons, and the best practices and procedures for making your turkey hunt a safe, responsible, and successful one. Turkey hunters need to

People with a yard near the woods can attract wild turkeys by planting trees with berries or nuts. But these can also attract squirrels and rodents, too.

have an array of information at hand. They need to follow local laws and regulations in order to hunt legally and ethically. Learning how to choose hunting sites is important, as is becoming familiar with weather patterns, mating season, and terrain. They need to learn techniques to outwit the bird's excellent vision and hearing. They must wear proper clothing, and learn how to blend into the surroundings. They have to be familiar with the different calls that will attract turkeys. And last but definitely not least is what to do with your wild turkey after it has been harvested.

Wild turkey populations are on the increase across North America due in large part to wildlife conservation and protection practices. Responsible hunting of wild turkeys keeps these populations healthy, and protects their feeding grounds. Conservation and management of wild areas is necessary not only to keep the continent beautiful, but also to nurture remote wilderness areas for generations to come.

Turkey hunting is one of the most enjoyable ways to exercise, enjoy time with others, and challenge yourself like your forebears have done. This guide will give you the tips, techniques, and strategies you need to make your hunting experiences ones to remember and cherish.

CHAPTER ONE

HUNTING FUNDAMENTALS

Hunting is serious business. Deadly weapons, human beings, and unpredictable animals can make for danger and even unintended lethal consequences. Each state or province has certain regulations that govern hunting and fishing in the area. The best place to start when you are thinking about hunting is a visit, either online or in person, to the local department of natural resources or department of game and wildlife to find information about the types of turkey hunting allowed during each season. Because wildlife is owned by the public, it's essential for hunters to follow the law.

Turkeys can be harvested with good hunting practices, stealth, proper weapons—and a bit of luck.

There are many websites that list the different hunting seasons for a chosen prey and that provide information about how to become a good hunter. When learning to hunt turkey or any prey, researching and using the proper gear and equipment is essential. One must develop persistence and patience, along with strong shooting skills, to become an accomplished hunter. Finally, it is important to understand that while the animal is the target, one must show respect for both the animal and nature.

A SACRED TRUST

As mentioned above, wildlife is a valuable, publicly owned resource. Therefore, it is important for hunters to consider wildlife management and conservation.

Wildlife management is a professional field in which people work to manage a population of wildlife in a certain area. Wildlife managers work to keep a population of wild animals, such as turkeys, at a desirable level. In their planning, managers must consider the capacity of the animal to reproduce and the factors that limit that capacity. Factors that limit a population's growth include loss of habitat, disease, predation, and hunter harvesting. Wildlife managers try to keep a balance between the factors that increase a population's growth and the factors that cut down a population's numbers.

Hunting in modern times is mainly for recreation, but it is also used to control the population. The different rules for the spring and fall hunting seasons are designed to help manage the wild turkey. During the spring hunting season, only toms (male turkeys) can be hunted. This helps to ensure the survival of the hens (female turkeys) that are breeding. During the fall hunting season, a hunter is able to hunt both hens and toms. There are also the following limits to wild turkey hunting in many places:

1. Strict bag limits (limits on the number of turkeys each hunter is able to harvest)

2. Limits on shooting hours
3. Banning of certain weapons and ammunition
4. Restrictions on the use of decoys and blinds
5. Prohibitions on the use of electronic calls

It is important to understand the local hunting regulations and rules before going turkey hunting. Hunters should check the rules in their county since the rules can be different from county to county.

Another part of wildlife management is managing land to improve wildlife habitats. By improving the land, wildlife managers create a place for turkeys and other wild animals to flourish, as well as a place for hunters to pass on their traditions.

THE CHOICE TO HUNT

People have many reasons for hunting. Some feel that it is a rite of passage that can significantly affect a person. They believe hunting can be a life-changing experience, giving young adults confidence and a sense of pride. Hunting can also be time well spent with family and friends. For many, getting together and going turkey hunting is a yearly tradition. John Ferguson, an expert turkey hunter in the New England area said, "One of my most exciting hunts was taking my twelve-year-old niece out for her very first hunt. We didn't even hear a bird gobble the first day, but she shot her first tom at 8:30 A.M. the next morning. I think I was more excited than she was. It [hunting] provides great times and memories."

People also hunt for food. If a hunter is lucky enough to harvest a wild turkey, the prize is the meat that the animal offers. The meat of wild game is much leaner than meat from farm-raised animals and is free of antibiotics and growth hormones.

Dogs have been hunting companions for thousands of years. Springer spaniels, like the one shown here, make good hunting dogs, as do Labrador retrievers, foxhounds, and beagles.

This is important to many people, who are concerned about the sources and quality of their food.

Some people hunt turkey for sport, or for the challenge of it. Others see hunting as a stress reliever and a way to relax. Hunting can take one away from the busyness of life. When hunting turkeys, a person typically walks alone in the woods. He or she is forced to be as quiet as possible and just listen to the sounds of nature. In this serene environment, a person can be alone with one's thoughts. The sport also allows one to peek into the lives of wild animals and view them in their element.

AN IMPORTANT RESOURCE

The National Wild Turkey Federation (NWTF) has played a large role in managing the wild turkey in the United States. This nonprofit conservation and hunting organization helps private landowners to manage wildlife on their property. The organization uses licensing fees from hunters, along with fundraising, to provide money to manage the turkey population. Some of the funds have been used for trap-and-release stocking programs. In these programs, turkeys are trapped in one place and then released in another place, where the turkey population is lower or the habitat is better suited to the birds.

Hunting seasons have been established in forty-nine US states, Canada, and Mexico thanks to the efforts of state, federal, and provincial wildlife agencies, as well as the NWTF and its partners. While wild turkey restoration is nearing completion, the NWTF still has much work to do. Across North America, supporters are working to enhance habitats for wild turkeys and other wildlife. At the same time, they are working to provide hunters with more opportunities and greater access to public and private land.

When the NWTF was established in 1973, there were only 1.3 million wild turkeys. That number peaked at 6.7 million turkeys in 2013. Since then, the number has fluctuated between 6 and 6.2 million birds throughout North America. While this may be a temporary decline, the federation is keeping a close eye on the population.

CONSERVING TURKEYS FOR TOMORROW

Wildlife conservation is the act of protecting, preserving, and studying wildlife and wildlife resources. The U.S. Fish and Wildlife Service (USFWS) reports that the primary source of funding for states' wildlife conservation efforts is the sale of hunting licenses, tags, and stamps. According to the bureau, when a hunter respects the hunting seasons, purchases all required licenses, and

Parents often pass along their skills and enjoyment of hunting to their children, who in turn may keep the tradition in the family with their own children.

pays federal excise taxes on hunting equipment, the hunter helps to ensure the future of many species and their habitats. The federal excise tax on hunting equipment raises about two hundred million dollars a year for conservation programs. These programs benefit both hunted and non-hunted wildlife species.

Local hunting clubs and national conservation organizations also work to protect the future of wildlife. According to the USFWS, such groups have set aside thousands of acres of habitat and have pushed for stronger conservation efforts in our national and state capitols. Some interesting clubs and organizations to check out are listed in the back of this book. An aspiring hunter can visit an organization's website, or become a member, to learn about hunting and how it affects the land and the extraordinary wildlife around us.

CHAPTER TWO

HANDLING WEAPONS

Whether you are a long-time handler of weapons or a complete beginner, it is crucial for you to either start or repeat training classes: lives could be at risk—including yours.

It is easy to become complacent around weapons, and dangerous. Turkeys can be taken down with firearms and/or archery, so the first decision is to choose which you will use for your hunt. All new skills require time and energy in the form of attention to detail and lots of practice, in order for you to achieve proficiency.

RESEARCH IS FUNDAMENTAL

If a person wants to become educated about turkey hunting, there are many places to go to get reliable information without having to spend a lot of money. Most local libraries have books and magazines about hunting in general and turkey hunting specifically. It costs no money at all to get a library card. Internet research is also an excellent source of information. There is a plethora of sites about turkey hunting on the web. Go online and see if there are any hunting safety courses in your area. A

Practicing shooting rifles and other firearms at shooting ranges helps hunters to familiarize themselves with their weapons in a safe, controlled setting.

good place to look is wherever hunting licenses are purchased in your region. Also, talk to local hunters. They can give you a firsthand perspective on hunting wild turkey and tell you exactly what you need to do to prepare for hunting.

SAFETY: THE FIRST PRIORITY

In order to handle a firearm safely, a person must respect the gun and treat every firearm as if it were loaded. One should never remove the gun's safety until the turkey is positively identified. A hunter should never point a gun at anything he or she is not planning to shoot. In addition, a hunter should not point a firearm in an unsafe direction, such as toward a person, a road, homes, or other buildings. Also, it is illegal for a person to discharge a firearm within 500 feet (152.4 meters) of any dwelling unless the hunter is the owner or has the owner's permission.

It is essential to know the location of one's target and what is behind the target. A missed shot from a shotgun can send stray ammunition traveling many yards beyond the intended target. Another rule is that a hunter should never shoot at a sound. One should always have a visual image and know exactly what one is shooting. If a person is not completely sure, he or she should not shoot.

TARGET PRACTICE

In order to be a responsible hunter, a person must get proper training in handling one's firearm, as well as a lot of practice shooting. If a person wants to learn how to shoot, he or she needs to understand and practice the rules of firearms safety. When target shooting, always remember to wear both eye and ear protection. It is imperative to follow the rules of the range where one is practicing.

Target shooting is divided into three "disciplines," according to the type of firearms used:

1. **Shotgun.** A semi-automatic or pump firearm for short-range shots.
2. **Rifle.** A firearm designed to be fired from the shoulder.
3. **Handgun.** A firearm designed to be held and operated using one hand.

Introductory classes at the range will help you decide which shooting discipline you like best. Young adults will find it is both challenging and fun to develop skills in concentration, hand-eye coordination, and precision. Firing ranges have specially designed targets for practicing these skills. Some are

Firearms are costly and dangerous investments. Obtaining the guidance of a professional retailer can help you choose the right weapon for you.

moving and some are static, or standing still. Targets are also located at different distances.

Once you determine the disciplines and games you enjoy most, your local sporting goods retailer can help you gear up with the right equipment. Finding a firearm with the right fit, as well as one that is appropriate for turkey hunting, will make for a safer hunting experience. In many places, turkey hunters are only allowed to shoot turkeys using a shotgun. A knowledgeable retailer can help a hunter find the right ammunition for the firearm. The retailer can also direct one to the correct safety equipment, including any mandatory eye and ear protection. The investment one makes in equipment will depend on how active or involved he or she wants to be.

More than nineteen million Americans safely participate in target shooting. The more target shooting an aspiring hunter does, the more prepared the person will be when he or she is hunting live turkeys out in the field.

SHOPPING FOR SHOTGUNS

Due to turkey hunting's popularity, there are a vast assortment of new and improved shotguns that have been designed specifically for turkey hunting. The following are some features to consider when selecting a shotgun and ammunition:

- **The vast majority of turkey hunters hunt with a 12-gauge shotgun, which comes in a variety of different makes and models.**
- **A modern turkey shotgun often comes with a camouflage finish.**
- **A shotgun with a shorter barrel will be lighter and more maneuverable.**
- **A shotgun with a longer barrel allows the hunter to shoot at a greater distance from the target.**
- **Some shot sizes and shell lengths are unique to turkey hunting. The best ammunition delivers a dense, hard-hitting pattern at a distance of 40 to 45 yards (37–41 m).**

Overall, the most important feature to confirm when selecting a shotgun is that the hunter can shoot it both comfortably and accurately.

FIREARM TRANSPORTATION

A hunter needs to transport and carry a gun from home to the hunting area. A number of states prohibit the carrying of uncased, loaded, long guns in a motor vehicle. Game wardens in many states strictly enforce regulations regarding the transportation of firearms during hunting season. As soon as any firearm—handgun, rifle, or shotgun—is carried on or about the person, or placed where it is readily accessible in a vehicle, state and local firearms laws regarding carrying apply. Some states have laws about carrying bows and crossbows as well. For up-to-date information on the laws and regulations in your state, visit the NRA's Institute for Legislative Action webpage at http://www.nraila.org/gun-laws.

BOW AND ARROW HUNTING

Some hunters enjoy using a bow and arrow when turkey hunting. The hunter must take good care of the archery equipment and handle it safely. By doing this, the hunter can ensure that everything works when it's time to hunt.

Just as when one is using a firearm, one should never point a bow at something that is not being targeted. A hunter should also never leave arrows on the string when he or she is not hunting or practicing.

When transporting archery equipment, it's a good idea to keep the bow and arrows in an archery case. This keeps the items from getting banged around when they are not in use. Don't leave the arrows knocked (on the bowstring) when transporting the archery equipment. Before putting archery equipment away, make sure that any moisture has been properly wiped off the bow. Moisture can lead to rust. It's also a good idea to use bowstring wax to keep the string in good shape when the equipment is not in use.

When carrying a bow, keep it at the side or in the front of the body to make sure it does not bang into anything. Doing this will prevent one from damaging the equipment and also from making noise. If a person's arm gets tired carrying the bow, a bow handle strap can be used. This is strapped over the hand, allowing the hunter to relax his or her grip and hold the bow longer. A professional at an archery store can show you other handy tools that help hunters carry a bow for long periods of time.

PRACTICE MAKES PERFECT

A good bow hunter must practice, practice, practice! One should spend a lot of

The familiar appearance of a target, with concentric rings, may date back to the 1400s. Coiled straw mats also serve as effective and reusable targets.

time learning how the bow works and using a target before going into the field. Taking a hunter safety course is an excellent way to learn archery basics. Many communities offer youth archery classes to make sure young people know the equipment and the rules.

When selecting a bow, make sure to choose one that is right for one's body size and strength. The weight of bow (when the bow is drawn in) should be comfortable. In addition, many bows can be adjusted to a hunter's draw length. The draw length is the length of the string when it is pulled back. Everyone has a different draw length, because everyone's arms are different sizes.

Chris Wiger was in fifth grade when he made a perfect score at the Minnesota State Indoor Archery Championships. Out of sixty shots in the inner ring, forty-five were bullseyes.

For advice on how to stand, how to hold your arms, and how to release the arrow, one should talk to an archery hunter. One important point to remember is this: Stay relaxed. Being nervous will make a hunter's body jerk and interfere with one's ability to hit the target. Experienced hunters and archery teachers can work with you to fine-tune your abilities.

DIFFERENCES BETWEEN ARCHERY AND FIREARM HUNTING

According to John Ferguson, avid turkey hunter in New England, some people believe it is easier to hunt with a gun than with a bow. However, regardless of which one you choose, you still need to be fairly close to your target. Ferguson said, "You must use a shotgun or bow, which limits your effective range to around 30 to 40 yards depending on your abilities." It is very difficult to hunt turkeys with a bow without the use of a ground blind, a camouflage tent that covers the hunter. Turkeys see movement very well. With eyes on the sides of their heads, a turkey can see a full 360 degrees.

Rob Elliot, an avid bow hunter, stated that he is licensed to hunt turkeys but has chosen not to because of their amazing eyesight. He said, "Many times when I have been bow hunting for deer I have scared turkeys away—and I was hundreds of yards away from them! I figured out that I would need to become much better at being quiet in the woods before I would be up to the challenge of turkey hunting." All of the senses other than smell and taste are finely tuned in the turkey. If a turkey hunter's heart is set on using a bow and arrow, one must learn how to shoot accurately and move quietly.

CHAPTER THREE

TURKEYS AND HUNTERS

Laws and regulations serve a vital function: they protect the public, the environment, other hunters, and property. Because laws and regulations are different in every state it is essential to check your local department of natural resource's website carefully. Not only do hunters have legal responsibilities to uphold, but ethical ones as well. Local hunting offices and officials can also be a good source of advice about what types of turkeys are in your area and which areas you are allowed to hunt them in.

KNOW THE LAW

Most states require that hunters take courses in order to receive a license to hunt. For instance, in the state of New York, a ten-hour hunter education course is mandatory. In cases in which a person has taken a course and then moves to another state, some states will honor education certificates and sporting licenses from other states and countries. There may be an additional course required for those hunters who would like to bow hunt. In some states, children under the age of twelve cannot obtain a hunting license or hunt wildlife. Age restrictions vary from state to state.

Flocks of wild turkeys can range in size from five to fifty individuals that can cover a home range of more than 1,000 acres (405 hectares).

There are different hunting seasons for different types of wildlife. Most states allow hunters to hunt wild turkeys in both the fall and the spring. However, there are often restrictions about the date ranges and areas in which you may hunt. Be sure to check dates and area restrictions on the local department of natural resources website.

A hunter must have personal identification, such as a license, permit, tag, or stamp, which can only be used by the person to whom it is issued. Be sure to check that the license has all of the correct information, since any errors can make the license invalid. Some states require that back tags be visibly displayed in the middle of the back while hunting.

KNOW YOUR DUTIES

Turkey hunters have legal and ethical responsibilities when it comes to harvesting a wild turkey. A hunter must always respect the laws and regulations that have been enacted to protect and maintain the wild turkey and its habitat.

Legal hunting means that a hunter has the proper licenses or permits to hunt wild turkeys. As stated before, the licensing fees for hunting help to support wildlife conservation programs. Legally, one must show his or her license if a law enforcement officer or property owner demands to see it. It is illegal to use another person's license, permit, or stamp while hunting unless the person named on the license is present.

Having a license does not give the holder the right to go on a person's private property to hunt, unless he or she has the permission of the landowner. It is illegal to trespass on private property in order to hunt. In other words, one cannot enter or pass through the property without the agreement of the owner.

Being an ethical hunter means respecting the animals one is hunting, as well as respecting nature and other hunters. One must follow the rules of fair chase and the laws of the area in which he or she is hunting. In addition, a hunter must be proficient with his or her weapon to ensure quick and clean kills. Further, if an animal is wounded, an ethical hunter will exhaust every means necessary to recover the animal.

According to John Ferguson, a responsible hunter does not take questionable shots. He or she must always be 100 percent sure of the target before pulling the trigger. Otherwise, unnecessary accidents can occur. The International Hunter Education Association website (http://www.ihea-usa.org) gives current statistics on the number of hunting accidents that occur in the United States.

It may be tempting to shoot turkeys so close to the fence, but you are risking fines and worse if you disobey the law.

DIFFERENCES BETWEEN PRIVATE AND PUBLIC LAND

Check the local department of natural resources or department of environmental conservation for private land locations and regulations for your state. There are many states that rely on private landowners for outdoor recreation. According to the New York State Department of Environmental Conservation (NYSDEC), since 85 percent of the state is privately owned, many hunters practice the sport on private property. The department's website (http://www.dec.ny.gov) states, "Nearly two-thirds of the hunting in New York State is on private lands and more than 90 percent of all hunters will hunt on private lands during the hunting seasons."

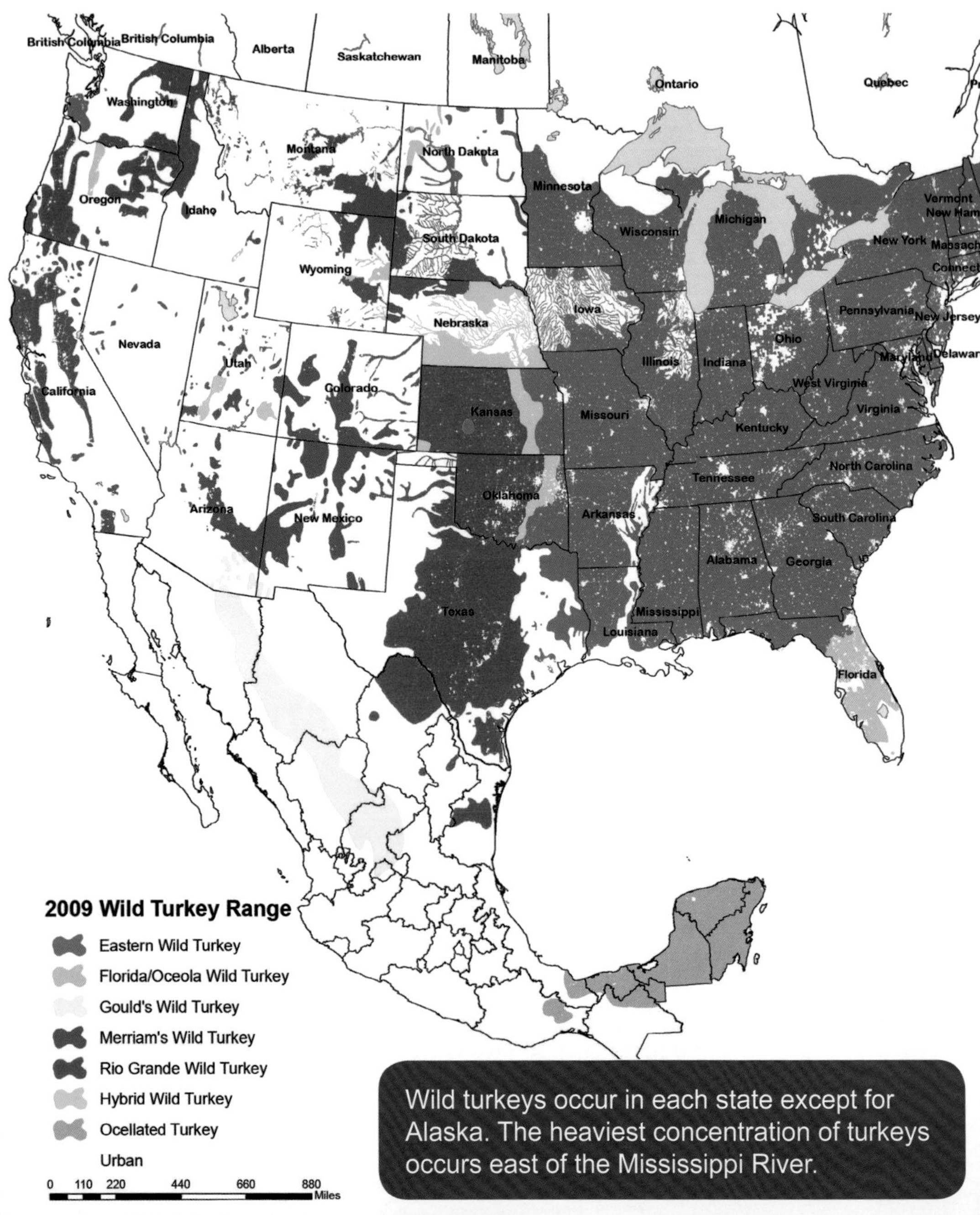

Wild turkeys occur in each state except for Alaska. The heaviest concentration of turkeys occurs east of the Mississippi River.

The NYSDEC gives a number of recommendations related to hunting on private land. First, as a responsible hunter, one must always seek permission prior to hunting on private land. This is true even if the land is not "posted," or marked with a warning sign that says no hunting or trespassing. The NYSDEC says that rural landowners are often willing to help hunters, if hunters demonstrate courtesy to them and respect for their property. If, however, trespassing, littering, and vandalism occur, access will likely be denied to visitors. It is also important to note that disturbing any trees or plants on private land without the permission of the landowner is illegal. Finally, a hunter should always find a way to thank a landowner for granting permission to be on his or her land. For example, one could offer to share his or her game or to buy some of the landowner's crops.

Many states have public lands available for hunting and trapping during the appropriate seasons. To find information about the hunting opportunities and rules for public land, contact the regional office of the department of environmental conservation or department of natural resources for the county in which one desires to hunt. Staff can provide information about cooperative hunting areas and wildlife management areas. Some states require written permission or permits, which can be obtained from the regional office.

TURKEY SPECIES IN NORTH AMERICA

The Eastern turkey is the most abundant and widespread turkey species. There are more than five million of these birds inhabiting the eastern, southern, and midwestern states, from Maine to Missouri. These turkeys live in diverse habitats such as forests in the Northeast, swamps in the South, and farmlands in the Midwest. The prime habitats for growing flocks are forests that are interspersed with fields, creeks, and rivers. The Eastern turkey roosts high up in the trees and across the flatlands. During poor weather, they seek warmth and shelter in evergreens. In the spring, gobblers (male turkeys) strut in open terrain, where hens are feeding and nesting.

The Osceola turkey range includes Florida, Georgia, and Louisiana. Osceola turkeys tend to roost in moss-laden cypress trees that grow in or on the edges of swamps, ponds, or creeks. During the fall, a hunter can find this species feeding in cattle pastures and burns. When springtime comes, these turkeys not only feed, but also strut and breed.

The Merriam's turkey is a species with approximately three hundred thousand to five hundred thousand birds. These turkeys inhabit fifteen Western states including South Dakota, Idaho, and New Mexico. In Canada, the birds live in Manitoba and Alberta in small populations. Merriam's turkeys inhabit timbered prairies, grasslands, scrub-oak and pine foothills, and mountains. During the spring and summer, these birds live up near snow-capped peaks. In the fall and winter, they migrate to lower elevations. Springtime means that gobblers are strutting for hens in mountain meadows or in grasslands near ponderosa pine roosts.

The Rio Grande turkey can be found in the Southcentral Plains. About one million Rios inhabit thirteen Plains and Western states. Eighty-five percent of America's Rio Grande flock roams the Lone Star State, where they are dubbed "Texas wild turkeys." Rio Grande turkeys typically roost in cottonwood, sycamore, and hackberry trees. Sometimes the turkeys will roost adjacent to grain fields, along streams, or in the tallest live oak. In the fall, it is not uncommon to find one hundred or more birds packed into a single tight stand of big trees. In the spring, twenty or more long-bearded toms, along with gaggles of hens and immature gobblers called "jakes," might roost side by side in tall oaks or cottonwoods. Male Rios strut all over the place in their open habitat during the spring mating season. Many gobblers also enjoy sections of crop fields or pastures near creeks or other water sources. This is especially true if there are good hen-nesting habitats, with low brush or other horizontal cover, close by.

The Gould's turkey inhabits the mountains of northwestern Mexico. In addition, several hundred Gould's turkeys currently roam mountain ranges in southern Arizona and New Mexico. This turkey is known as a mountain bird, living in southwestern hills that range from 4,500 feet (1,372 m) to more than 7,000 feet (2,134 m) in elevation. The turkey's habitat is laced with steep, rough, and rocky canyons and drainages. Pinion pines and scrub oaks in the canyon bottoms provide Gould's turkeys with good food, roost trees, and nesting and security cover.

Some turkey hunters try to achieve the "grand slam" of turkey hunting. To do this, the hunter must harvest one of each of the North American species of turkey within a set period of time. Some try to reach this goal in one season or over a period of years.

PECULIARITIES OF TURKEYS

Many people don't know that turkeys have excellent vision. They have the ability to twist their heads 360 degrees, so they can see all the way around. If you can see a turkey's head, the turkey can see you. A turkey's eyes are set in the sides of its head for monocular vision. Each eye is used separately, increasing the turkey's field of view. However, while turkeys see 20/20 during the day, they do have poor night vision. Turkeys also have extremely sharp hearing. This makes it hard for the hunter: the turkey can hear the slightest of sounds, from the slapping of brush to the clicking of safety on a shotgun. This is because the ear flaps work to funnel in sound waves. On the other hand, turkeys are known to have a poor sense of smell. Also, turkeys are believed to have relatively few taste buds.

When a turkey senses that it is in danger, it will run with a tremendous amount of energy and quickness. The turkey will tuck its head low to the ground and tear off into the brush. Turkeys have strong and muscular legs, which are good for running and launching into the air. Turkeys are skittish creatures that are unpredictable with their movements. Something as simple as the shadow of another animal is enough to spook, or scare, a turkey. These qualities make the turkey hunter's job quite challenging.

CHAPTER FOUR

LOGISTICS OF THE HUNT

Turkeys are easily spooked, which means that they can be unpredictable. Their excellent vision can allow them to notice inconsistencies in the environment, even something as small as white earmuffs protruding from under a hood! Hunters need to plan ahead so that they can take advantage of the full range of information available for a successful hunt. Like the Boy Scouts of America, your motto should be Be Prepared.

BEFORE THE HUNT

Scouting before hunting season involves taking the time to see where the wild turkeys are gathering. This is important preparation for the actual hunt: a hunter will be much more efficient with information about where all the turkeys are. One should hike around the hunt zones a month or so before the season starts.

When scouting, look for tracks and scats (droppings). There is a noticeable difference in the appearance of a hen's and a gobbler's tracks and scats. Checking local library resources and going online are great ways to research turkey tracks and scats. Also, as opening day approaches, walk and or drive around and

Wild turkeys do not hunt at night. Instead, at dusk they find roosts to sleep in, usually in trees.

listen for gobbles. Mark the areas where you hear the sounds on a map to remember where to go when it is time to hunt.

TURKEY SOUNDS

When listening for the wild turkey, it is important to know that different turkeys make different sounds. An excited hen makes a series of fast, loud, erratic single notes; this is known as "cutting." A typical gobble from a gobbler or tom lasts for about two to three seconds. An older tom will have a deep, full-throated gobble. A jake, or young male, has a short gobble; it has not yet developed the ability to fully gobble. Wild turkeys are very vocal in the late winter and early spring. A hunter will hear yelping, cutting, gobbling, purring, and other sounds.

The website of the National Wildlife Federation (http://www.nwf.org) is just one of the many sites that allow hunters to listen to the different sounds and become familiar with them. Then, when hunting, the turkey sounds will be recognizable. Hunters use turkey calls to simulate the different sounds and draw in wild turkeys. For example, a hunter can make the sound of a hen to attract a tom.

Once a hunter gets a tom to gobble, he or she shouldn't "overcall" the turkey, or bother it with too many calls. One should let the tom gobble a few times between calls because the tom is trying to call the hen (who is really the hunter). If the tom stops gobbling, the hunter should stop calling altogether. This may make the turkey come to look for him or her. Sometimes a tom will gobble a few times and then approach silently. A hunter should be patient and shouldn't give up too early on a bird. A lack of gobbling doesn't necessarily mean the tom is not coming. Sometimes it helps to use a decoy to direct the turkey's attention elsewhere. When the hunter is ready to shoot, he or she can remove the safety on the weapon and fire.

The National Wild Turkey Federation website (http://www.nwtf.org) is another place to listen to each of the different turkey calls. Here are just a few of the sounds that wild turkeys make:

- **Cluck.** One or more short, staccato notes, usually used by one bird to get the attention of another.
- **Putt.** This sound signals danger to other birds. It indicates that a turkey has seen or heard something that it doesn't like. It can be a single note or several sharp, rapid notes.
- **Tree call.** A series of soft, muffled yelps that is made by a

roosted bird. It is used as a way to communicate with others in the flock.

- **Gobble.** This sound is made by the male wild turkey. It is primarily used during the springtime to let hens know he is in the vicinity.
- **Yelp.** A series of single-note vocalizations. A yelp can have different meanings, depending on the way the hen uses it.

It is helpful to be familiar with a variety of turkey calls. Using just one of these calls may not always work to draw in a turkey. The more calls you know, the better you will be at hunting. Here are some examples of turkey calls that hunters use:

- **Diaphragm call.** This air-activated device consists of latex reeds, an aluminum frame or frames, and a skirt. A hunter makes turkey sounds by pushing air through the diaphragm call and forming the mouth to say certain words. The diaphragm call is the most popular call but the hardest to master.
- **Slate Call.** To make sounds, a hunter pulls a striker across a circular surface that is made out of slate, glass, aluminum, or a combination of these materials. Most beginners can pick up this call very quickly.
- **Box Call.** A hunter simply slides a wooden lid across an open box to create the sound. This is one of the easiest calls to learn.

HUNTING IN SPRING AND FALL

According to John Ferguson, spring turkey hunting is exciting, challenging, and fast paced. In springtime, hunters can harvest only toms. To call in a male, or "tom turkey," the hunter needs to mimic a hen, because this is the breeding season. This is achieved by using diaphragm calls, slate calls, or wooden box calls. It takes practice to become proficient with these calls. One wrong sound can be the difference between harvesting a turkey and going home empty handed. It is possible to call a tom from over half a mile (805 m) away. Sometimes a bird will come in within a few minutes. Other times a hunter will have to work with a turkey for hours.

During the fall hunting season, a hunter is allowed to take either male or female turkeys. The hunter needs to be well concealed because the key is to try to ambush the birds at their food sources. Turkeys are only concerned with feeding and staying alive in the fall, so food sources and roosting areas (sleeping

Female turkeys, or hens, have a separate "pecking order" from males. Both sexes fight for dominance.

areas) are the best places to scout. If a hunter scatters a flock in the fall, he or she can usually use soft clucks to bring the birds back in. A hunter is not able to shoot a turkey that is on roost, but must wait until the turkey is on the ground.

GETTING IN SHAPE

When preparing for turkey hunting, one must not only have the proper training and equipment, but must also be in good physical condition. There are many ways a person can prepare for the physical demands of hunting. For example, one can exercise on a daily basis and practice healthy eating habits.

It is also important for a hunter to be aware of his or her physical limitations. Many hunting injuries or deaths are actually due to hunters having heart attacks or suffering heat stroke because they were not used to the physical exertion of hunting. This applies more frequently to older adults. However, as a young hunter, it is a good idea to get in shape now and to build healthy habits. Some hunters wisely spend a few weeks before hunting season in the gym or outdoors, building up their endurance and strength.

KEEPING SAFE

When turkey hunting, there is a proper way for a hunter to sit and wait for a turkey. The guidelines include the following rules: First, it is essential that the hunter does not load the gun until he or she is set up and is calling the turkey in. Whenever you can hear another hunter working a bird, do not go in that area at all. If you are not completely sure that you are the only one working

PACKING LIST OF ITEMS TO BRING ALONG ON A TURKEY HUNT

- **Bug repellant**
- **Call tuning kit**
- **Compact binoculars**
- **GPS**
- **Cushion**
- **Extra shells**
- **First aid kit**
- **Flashlight**
- **Knife/multi-tool**
- **Orange cap (for after the shot)**
- **Pocket camera**
- **Water and snacks**
- **Rain gear**
- **Warm hat**
- **Gun or bow**
- **Hunting license**

in a bird, do not take any chances. It is never worth taking a risk if you or someone else may get hurt.

Yelping while one is on the move in the woods can also be detrimental. Another hunter may hear the sound and mistake it for a wild turkey. His or her adrenaline can kick in and lead to an accident. Sit still and spend some time really seeing your surroundings and listening for signs of hunters. Before raising a gun or bow, be absolutely sure that it is a turkey you are hunting and not another person. If another hunter is visible, let him or her know by giving a loud and firm "Good morning!" or by saying, "It's a beautiful day out!" Wait to show yourself until the other person's gun is down and he or she is relaxed. After shooting a turkey, place it in an orange vest or carrying bag so that other hunters see a bag and not a wild turkey moving.

WHAT TO WEAR

As a hunter one needs to be concerned about camouflage as well as comfort, silence, safety, and warmth. Expert turkey

Turkeys' keen eyesight makes it necessary for hunters to choose camouflage clothing carefully.

hunter Ben Cowan says that he lives by two clothing rules when hunting in the woods: First, purchase quiet fabric that provides comfort from the elements and mosquitoes. Second, remember to think about everything from your undergarments to pieces that will cover you from head to toe.

A hunter's undergarments should be made from modern synthetic fabrics, which wick away moisture and keep a hunter warm. Purchasing green, brown, or camouflage long johns will ensure that no light colors pop out from underneath clothing. For outerwear, a hunter should wear full camouflage, including coverage for the hands and face. Turkeys have excellent vision. Pants should have enough length that legs are covered when one is sitting with the knees drawn up.

Many hunters consider the vest the most important article of clothing because it works like both a suitcase and a filing cabinet. It provides storage for calls and other various tools needed while hunting. Some vests have a cushion seat attached for comfort when sitting for long periods of time.

Head and face coverings are also key items. A hunter should wear a face mask so that he or she will not expose a shiny forehead or rosy cheeks. Wild turkeys will pick up on such details with their keen eyesight. When the weather is hot, one can wear a camouflage baseball cap with mesh. Gloves should also be camouflage and should have long, knit wrists. Make sure that the gloves are thin so hands can be used to give calls, release the safety on a gun, pull a trigger, or shoot a bow.

A turkey hunter's footwear depends on the season. Tall rubber boots with good cushioning and foot support are great for rainy weather. Insulated leather boots work well when the weather is cold. Good, waterproof hiking boots can also keep the feet warm. A thin pair of polypropylene liner socks combined with wool outer socks will help to wick away moisture and keep the feet dry and comfortable.

CHAPTER FIVE

STRATEGIES, TECHNIQUES, AND MORE

Hunters heading out for a hunt have a lot of decisions to make. What season is it? What is the weather like? Will they be hunting alone, or with a group? Depending on the answers to these questions hunters can use different techniques and strategies. After a hunter succeeds in harvesting a turkey, there are procedures that need to be followed to ensure that the turkey is prepared properly. Perhaps the hunter wants to keep the turkey as a trophy. If so, that should be planned for. Hunting can be a strenuous experience, time-consuming and challenging. The more a hunter prepares, the better the trip will be.

HUNTING IN THE QUIET

Still-hunting involves slowly and quietly stalking an animal. The best time to use this hunting tactic is when the weather is rainy and the ground is wet and soft. The moist land absorbs the sound of footsteps, allowing the hunter to stalk in a quieter fashion. According to http://www.warriorcritic.com, "The best technique for still-hunting is to move slowly and methodically throughout the woods. Walk short distances as quietly as possible.

Imitating the sounds of birds has long been a tactic of hunters. Different styles of turkey calls can be found in your local sporting goods store.

Stop and look around the area thoroughly before moving on." Excess movement is not recommended when turkey hunting. A person's movements will spook the bird and send it running in the other direction.

TEAM HUNTING

Group hunts can be fun because it is time spent with others doing an activity everyone enjoys. It is also an opportunity to learn from others with more experience or to teach someone

Hunters who stalk prey in groups need to be careful to note the location of every member of their party.

who is new to the sport. Hunt with someone with whom you get along. You can hunt with someone who has the same hunting style or someone who knows techniques that you would like to learn.

Choose one person to be in charge of the hunt so there is no confusion when everyone is out in the field. Always be aware of your hunting partners' locations. Also, be sure to establish silent hand signals before the hunt. Any talking in the woods will scare the turkeys.

WHEN BAD WEATHER HAPPENS

Hunting seasons cannot be extended due to bad weather. In order to make the best use of the available time, it is important to know what to do when conditions are not ideal.

When there is a lot of wind, it is very difficult to hear a turkey approaching. As a turkey hunter, one relies on close listening in order to locate the turkey. Find places with less wind, like valleys or the sides of a hill, which give some protection. Allow the wind to be at your back. That way, the wind will carry the sounds of the turkey to you.

A good pair of binoculars is necessary for viewing wildlife, whether you are hunting or just sightseeing.

In rainy conditions, turkeys are still active, even though the sun is not shining. The problem is that one cannot hear the hunter's call—or the turkeys—as well above the sound of the rain. Keep in mind that turkeys usually start gobbling right before and right after a storm. During the rain and after it has stopped, turkeys will often go out into the open fields. There, they can dry off and find protection from sneaky predators. Make sure the proper rain gear is close at hand. Otherwise, the rain could make for a miserable outing.

In snowy weather, a hunter must wear the proper attire. Realize your limitations, and don't allow frostbite to develop.

TACTICS FOR HUNTING IN A GROUP

Hunting with others can be enjoyable, especially when your efforts lead to success. The following are some strategies to try when hunting with a group:

- **Split up well before sunrise to listen in different directions for gobbles. Then meet up several minutes before sunrise to compare notes.**
- **One person can "yelp," while the other stays still and listens.**
- **Set up and work a gobbler side by side. Whisper to communicate with each other.**
- **Set up a system of nonverbal communication. Use hand signals or read one another's body language.**

Always be sure that the campsite is close enough that you will be able to make it back to your truck and/or camp. Turkeys may be quieter when there is snow, but against the white background, they are more visible to the hunter's eye.

Part of being a responsible hunter is being prepared for everything. Check the local forecast on TV, on the radio, or online. It is better to have more items with you than not enough. Layers can always be removed and stored at the campsite or in the truck.

PULLING THE TRIGGER

When setting up to take a shot at a turkey, do not attempt to get close to the roost. Patience is key. A hunter needs to sit still and quietly wait for the approaching bird. A responsible and ethical hunter will wait to take the right shot, so that the bird is cleanly harvested. When one spots the red, white, and blue head and the swinging beard of the turkey within about 40 yards (37 m), it is time to take the shot. A hunter using a shotgun looks behind the turkey for safety, waits for the turkey to extend its neck, and then shoots the base of the neck. A hunter using a bow aims for the body of the bird.

WHEN THE HARVEST IS SUCCESSFUL

After a hunter has harvested a turkey, there are some steps to follow to ensure proper preservation and the ability to consume the turkey. In order to field dress a turkey (one that will not be made into a full size-mount), the hunter places the turkey on its back wings. He or she moves the wings to the sides and points the legs up. The hunter inserts the tip of a knife at the bottom of the breastplate and cuts back to the anal vent. One proceeds to remove all of the entrails through this opening. Then, one removes the heart and lungs by reaching up into the cavity to sever the windpipe. The hunter uses a damp paper towel to clean blood from the feathers if there is a plan to have the bird mounted.

When transporting the turkey after the field dressing has taken place, a hunter tucks the prized turkey into a vest or carries it by the legs, not the neck. One must carry the bird with care, especially if it is going to be mounted. The hunter wraps an orange vest or an orange bag around the bird until it is placed in the vehicle. That way, another hunter won't mistake it for a live bird. One should put the bird on ice to keep it cool while transporting it. If the hunter is not able to get the turkey to a taxidermist right away, the bird is frozen.

A familiar dish during the holiday season, turkeys can be fried, roasted, or smoked for a delicious meal.

The next step is to skin the turkey. First, the hunter cuts through the skin from the chest to the anal vent. Starting at the neck, the hunter skins the bird, cutting the neck bone and flesh without cutting through the skin of the neck. The head remains attached to the skin of the neck, and the neck skin remains attached to the body skin. The hunter proceeds to skin down the back of bird toward the wings and legs. One dislocates the wing bone from the body. Then one works down to the legs and dislocates each leg from the body. The bones and the wings are left intact. The hunter disconnects the tail from the body, but leaves the tail attached to the skin. Then one completely skins the back of the bird. One also tries to gently remove any blood from the feathers.

SAVING YOUR TURKEY FOR LATER

Taxidermy is a term for the variety of methods one uses to reproduce a lifelike, three-dimensional representation of an animal. A turkey hunter goes to a taxidermist so that the harvested turkey can be put up for permanent display. There are many ways that a hunter can have the turkey displayed.

A life-size mount can be in any position a hunter can imagine. In the most popular pose, a tom looks like it is gobbling on the roost while it hangs on the wall. Other options are the strutting pose or the standing pose. Another possibility is to do a half mount with just the chest, head, and fan of the bird. Taxidermists mount the turkey by taking the skin and slipping it over a foam-plastic body. A newer option is to place an artificial head and chest in front of the natural tail fanning out on a plaque.

Turkey hunting is a sport that one should enter with a lot of thought and research. A great deal of work goes into preparing for the actual hunt. A hunter can feel a great sense of pride and fulfillment when he or she is carrying the turkey home to be eaten and mounted. As a young adult, turkey hunting is a great way to learn patience and endurance, and to gain a greater respect for nature.

Here are some final pieces of advice: Find hunting companions that are enthusiastic and that have a lot of experience. Learning from the best will make a person a better hunter. Be sure to always practice safe hunting techniques, and value the whole experience of the hunt, not just the shot. Hunting ethically and responsibility will ensure a positive and safe experience, not only for the hunter, but also for the wild turkey.

GLOSSARY

array A large number.
blind A hiding place, similar to a tent, which is used by hunters.
breed To produce offspring.
capacity The ability to hold a certain number of people or things.
crucial Important.
decoy Something used to lure an animal so that it can be trapped or killed.
excise taxes Federal or state taxes imposed on the manufacture and distribution of certain nonessential consumer goods.
field dress Preparing the hunted animal for use in the field.
game warden A person who is employed to protect wildlife.
gobbler A male turkey.
habitat The surroundings or natural conditions in which a plant or animal lives.
hen A female turkey.
harvest To shoot, trap, or catch fish or game.
hunting season The season in which people are permitted to hunt.
imperative Not to be ignored or avoided.
jake Immature male turkey.
mandatory Required or commanded by authority.
monocular vision The kind of vision in which each eye is used separately.
personal identification A document that is shown to verify a person's identity.
predation The act of seizing and feeding upon prey.
proficiency An increase in skill or knowledge.
rite of passage A ritual or event that marks a person's move into the next stage of his or her life.

roost Place where a winged animal rests and sleeps.

scout To explore in order to gain information.

taxidermist A person who specializes in stuffing and mounting the skins of animals for display.

tom A male turkey.

tracks Marks or other discoverable evidence left by an animal.

wildlife conservation Planned protection, preservation, and study of wildlife and wildlife resources.

wildlife management The act of managing a population of animals.

FOR MORE INFORMATION

Canadian Shooting Sports Association (CSSA)
1143 Wentworth St. W. Unit 204
Oshawa, ON L1J 8P7
Canada
(888) 873-4339
Facebook: @cdnshootingsports
Website: http://www.cdnshootingsports.org
The CSSA supports and promotes all kinds of shooting sports, including hunting and archery, and works politically to fight for the rights of responsible Canadians to have unrestricted, lawful access to firearms.

Canadian Wild Turkey Federation
RR#1 215 Detroit Line
Wheatley, Ontario N0P 2P0
Canada
Website: https://cwtf.ca
Facebook: @canadianwildturkeyfederation
Twitter: @cwtfederation
Instagram: @canadianwildturkey
The federation exists to promote "the establishment, restoration, preservation, and sustainable management of wildlife and habitat in Canada, with a focus on wild turkeys."

National Rifle Association of America
11250 Waples Mill Road
Fairfax, VA 22030
(800) 672-3888
Website: https://firearmtraining.nra.org
Facebook/Instagram: @NationalRifleAssociation
Twitter: @NRA

The NRA's training and education department offers a number of programs across the US designed to teach shooters safe, ethical and responsible firearm practices.

National Shooting Sports Foundation (NSSF)
Flintlock Ridge Office Center
11 Mile Hill Road
Newtown, CT 06470-2359
(203) 426-1320
Website: http://www.nssf.org
Facebook: @nssfcomm
Twitter: @NSSF
Instagram: @thenssf
The National Shooting Sports Foundation (NSSF) is the trade association for the shooting, hunting, and firearms industry. The NSSF is a nonprofit organization that promotes, protects, and preserves hunting and the shooting sports.

National Wild Turkey Federation
PO Box 530
Edgefield, SC 29824-0530
(800) 843-6983
Website: http://www.nwtf.org
Facebook: @thenwtf
Twitter: @nwtf_official
Instagram: @official_nwtf
The National Wild Turkey Federation is a national nonprofit conservation and hunting organization that, along with its volunteers, partners, and sponsors, works for the conservation and preservation of the wild turkey.

Professional Bowhunters Society
PO Box 246

Terrell, NC 28682
(704) 664-2534
Website: http://www.professionalbowhunters.org
Facebook: @169569076222
The Professional Bowhunters Society has been a strong force in the continuation of bowhunting. It is an organization of experienced bowhunters that values leadership and "knowledge through experience."

U.S. Fish & Wildlife Service
1849 C Street NW
Washington, DC 20240
(800) 344-9453
Website: http://www.fws.gov
Facebook/Twitter/Instagram: @usfws
The government agency that manages America's natural resources in order to conserve, protect, and enhance wildlife, plants, and their habitats.

FOR FURTHER READING

Graubart, Norman D. *How to Track a Turkey*. New York, NY: Windmill Books, 2015.

Hemstock, Annie. *Bow Hunting*. New York, NY: Rosen Publishing, 2015.

Hemstock, Annie. *Hunting Laws and Safety*. New York, NY: Rosen Publishing, 2015.

Hunt, Will. *Hunting Wild Turkeys: Getting Started*. Raleigh, NC: Monte Perron, 2016.

Kelly, Tom. *Tenth Legion "White Edition."* 40th anniversary ed. Spanish Fort, AL: Tom Kelly, Inc., 2012.

Lovett, Brian. *A Far Green Country*. Brian Lovett, CreateSpace: 2015.

Morgan, Kenny. *Turkey Hunting: A One Man Game*. College Station, TX: Morgan's Turkey Callers, 2016.

Pedersen, Cory. *Shawn Buckner's Outdoor Adventures: Spring Turkey Chronicles.* Amazon, 2012.

Pendergast, George. *Turkey Hunting*. New York, NY: Gareth Stevens Publishing, 2015.

Phillips, John E. *Mossy Oak Pros Talk Turkey Tactics*. Amazon, 2016.

BIBLIOGRAPHY

Bourjaily, Philip. *The Field & Stream Turkey Hunting Handbook* (Field & Stream Fishing and Hunting Library). Guilford, CT: Lyons Press, 1999.

Clancy, Gary. *Wild Turkey* (The Hunting and Fishing Library. Complete Hunter.) Minnetonka, MN: Creative Publishing, 1996.

Elliot, Robert. Email interview with author, January 17, 2010.

Eye, Ray. *Practical Turkey Hunting Strategies: How to Effectively Hunt Birds Under Any Conditions*. Guilford, CT: Lyons Press, 2003.

Ferguson, John. Email interview with author, January 15, 2010.

Hanback, Michael. *Advanced Turkey Hunting* (Complete Hunter). Chanhassen, MN: Creative Publishing, 2003.

Hunting Net, Inc. "Turkey History." http://www.huntingnet.com/articles/turkey-history.html.

Hunting Net, Inc. "Turkey Hunting – Safety." http://www.huntingnet.com/articles/turkey-hunting-safety.html.

Mettler, John J. *Wild Turkeys: Hunting and Watching.* Pownal, VT: Storey Books, 1998.

Miller, Derek. "Thanksgiving by the Numbers." Fox Business, November 23, 2016. http://www.foxbusiness.com/features/2016/11/23/thanksgiving-by-numbers.html.

New York State Department of Environmental Conservation. "Places to Hunt in New York." http://www.dec.ny.gov/outdoor/7844.html.

Sapir, Glenn. *Hunt Wild Turkey! Pros' Secrets for Success*. Minnetonka, MN: Shady Oak Press, 2008.

Trout, John. *The Complete Book of Wild Turkey Hunting: A Handbook of Techniques and Strategies*. Guilford, CT: Lyons Press, 2000.

U.S. Fish & Wildlife Service. "2016 National Survey of Fishing, Hunting, and Wildlife-Associated Recreation." August 2017. https://wsfrprograms.fws.gov/Subpages/NationalSurvey/nat_survey2016.pdf.

U.S. Fish & Wildlife Service. "USFWS – Hunting." http://www.fws.gov/hunting.

U.S. Fish & Wildlife Service. "What Do Hunters Do for Conservation?" March 4, 2014. http://www.fws.gov/hunting/whatdo.html.

INDEX

ABOUT THE AUTHORS

Xina M. Uhl has written a number of educational books for young people, in addition to textbooks, teacher's guides, lessons, and assessment questions. She has tackled subjects including sports, history, biographies, technology, and health concerns. Although she has friends and family who hunt, she shoots animals only through her camera lens. Her blog details her publications as well as interesting facts and the occasional cat picture.

Kate Canino is an author and educator currently living in Rochester, New York. A graduate of the College of Saint Rose, with a degree in childhood education, she is always trying ways to inspire kids to find ways to educate themselves and be active in hobbies they are interested in. She has many friends who enjoy turkey hunting, bowhunting, and target shooting and loves to hear their stories about what it's like to be out in the wilderness hunting for turkeys. She has two books published by Rosen Publishing, one on the health benefits of cycling for kids and the other on controlling weight and building healthy habits.

ABOUT THE CONSULTANT

Benjamin Cowan has over twenty years of both big game and small game hunting experience. In addition to being an avid hunter, Cowan is also a member of many conservation organizations. He currently resides in west Tennessee.

PHOTO CREDITS

Cover Paul Tessier/Shutterstock.com; back cover Drakuliren/Shutterstock.com; pp. 4–5 (background) Outdoor_Media/Shutterstock.com; p. 5 BestPhotoStudio/Shutterstock.com; pp. 7, 14, 24, 33, 43 Michael Tatman/Shutterstock.com; p. 7 John Wilton/EyeEm/Getty Images; p. 10 John P Kelly/The Image Bank /Getty Images; p. 12 Nikolay Gyngazov/Shutterstock; p. 15 Christie Richwalski/EyeEm/Getty Images; p. 17 nik wheeler/Corbis Documentary/Getty Images; pp. 20–21 Adie Bush/Image Source/Getty Images; p. 22 © AP Images; p. 25 Kelly/Getty Images; p. 27 Donald M. Jones/Minden Pictures/Getty Images; p. 28 Courtesy of the National Wild Turkey Foundation; p. 34 Paul Sparks/Shutterstock.com; p. 37 James Pintar/Shutterstock.com; pp. 40–41, 44 Mitch Kezar/Design Pics/Getty Images; p. 45 AndreyUG /Shutterstock.com; pp. 46–47 nathanmcc/Shutterstock.com; p. 50 Rick Poon/Moment/Getty Images.

Design: Michael Moy; Photo Research: Xina Uhl